For Molly and Catey

Luna Luna

Copyright © 2013 by Sam Ryan

Requests for permission to make copies of any part of the work should be submitted online at info@mascotbooks.com or mailed to Mascot Books, 560 Herndon Parkway #120, Herndon, VA 20170.

PRT0613A

Printed in the United States

ISBN-13: 9781620863527
ISBN-10: 1620863529

www.mascotbooks.com

Luna Luna

Sam Ryan

Illustrated by
Hazel Mitchell

Late, late one night, when even the nightingales had stopped their singing and it was very, very still, Roshi woke up from his faraway dreams to find a strange moon floating in the trees outside his window.

It was not a white, bright moon like the moon you see in pictures or the high, clear moon you see when the cold is chilling your nose on brisk fall nights. This moon was a misty summer moon, streaked with green and red and yellow and purple. It was a wonderful moon.

Roshi watched the moon for a long, long time from the safety of his warm, snuggly bed. Then, very quietly, he got up, hardly making a sound in the dim light, and tiptoed downstairs. Roshi didn't want to wake his sister or his parents.

Slowly, carefully, he opened the front door and slipped outside into the hazy blue night. He found what he was looking for – his net, resting against a big flowerpot along the wall.

Roshi looked up at the moon. And, as if that
moon were just another of the butterflies he had
tried to catch all that lazy summer afternoon,
he softly and quickly swung his net as high as he
could. It was a big swing, but he didn't come close
to catching the moon.

He thought the moon smiled at him from its
perch high and free in the deep night sky.

Roshi tried again . . . and again . . . and again. First
standing on the tips of his toes, then jumping
as high as he could. He even went over to the
twisted stump in the yard, climbed up, and swung
his net from there.

But it was no use. The moon looked down at him,
all green and red and yellow and purple, as if
nothing had happened. As if nothing would happen.

Roshi sat down on the porch and thought . . . and
watched . . . and thought . . . and watched. He
watched the moon float down through the trees on
the hill in front of the house. A hill, he thought.

In a flash, he was out the front gate, across the road, and up into the woods he knew so well. He climbed higher and higher, chasing the moon, which always seemed to be just ahead of him.

Every time Roshi came to a clearing, the moon smiled and beckoned him deeper into the night. Roshi would swing his net. But he could not catch the moon.

At last, Roshi reached the old pond fed by a
spring that gurgled from the side of the hill. He
listened to the trickling water as he sat down to
rest on an upside-down bucket. The moon rested,
too, in the pond.

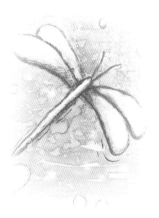

There, there was the moon, right beside him!
As quick as he could, Roshi plunged his net into
the water. But the moon vanished in a sparkling
splash. Bits of moon seemed to laugh at him in
the spreading ripples.

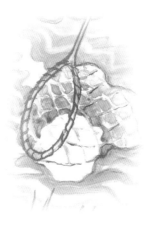

Eventually, the moon returned. This time, Roshi
was much more careful. Kneeling down, he slowly
lowered his net into the pond and slid it beneath
the moon.

With a cry of triumph, Roshi sprang to his feet,
yanking his net from the water. But the moon
slipped through the net and once more slid away
in the ripples.

"Aha," said Roshi, "the holes in my net are too large."

So he took the bucket and slowly, slowly scooped the whole moon out of the water. At last, the moon was in his pail. He had it! His green, red, yellow and purple moon stared back at him dimly from inside the bucket.

"I've got you, I've got you!" Roshi cried. And now it was Roshi who smiled, proud of himself for finally having caught the moon.

Carefully, so as not to spill his new treasure, Roshi started down the mountain, one eye watching the moonlit stones and bushes, one eye watching his bucket.

He was so happy he started to hum to himself an old song, "Luna, Luna."

Whither whither wandering Moon?
The night is ending much too soon,
The eastern sky glows pinkly blue,
And morning birds are chirping.

Luna, luna, slip away,
Luna, luna, never stay.

Roshi felt so warm inside, he didn't even notice
the tiny hole in the bottom of his bucket.

Drip, drip, drip.